Late for School

E
MAR

Grand Central Publishing
Hachette Book Group
237 Park Avenue
New York, NY 10017

www.HachetteBookGroup.com

Printed in Singapore

First Edition: September 2010
10 9 8 7 6 5 4 3 2 1

Grand Central Publishing is a division of Hachette Book Group, Inc.
The Grand Central Publishing name and logo is a trademark of Hachette Book Group, Inc.

ISBN: 978-044-6-55702-3
Library of Congress Control Number: 2009940755

Late for School

Steve Martin

Illustrated by C. F. Payne

GC

GRAND CENTRAL
PUBLISHING

NEW YORK   BOSTON

Woke up this morning
Clock said I was late for school
Teacher told me that's not cool
Gotta put my shirt and pants on

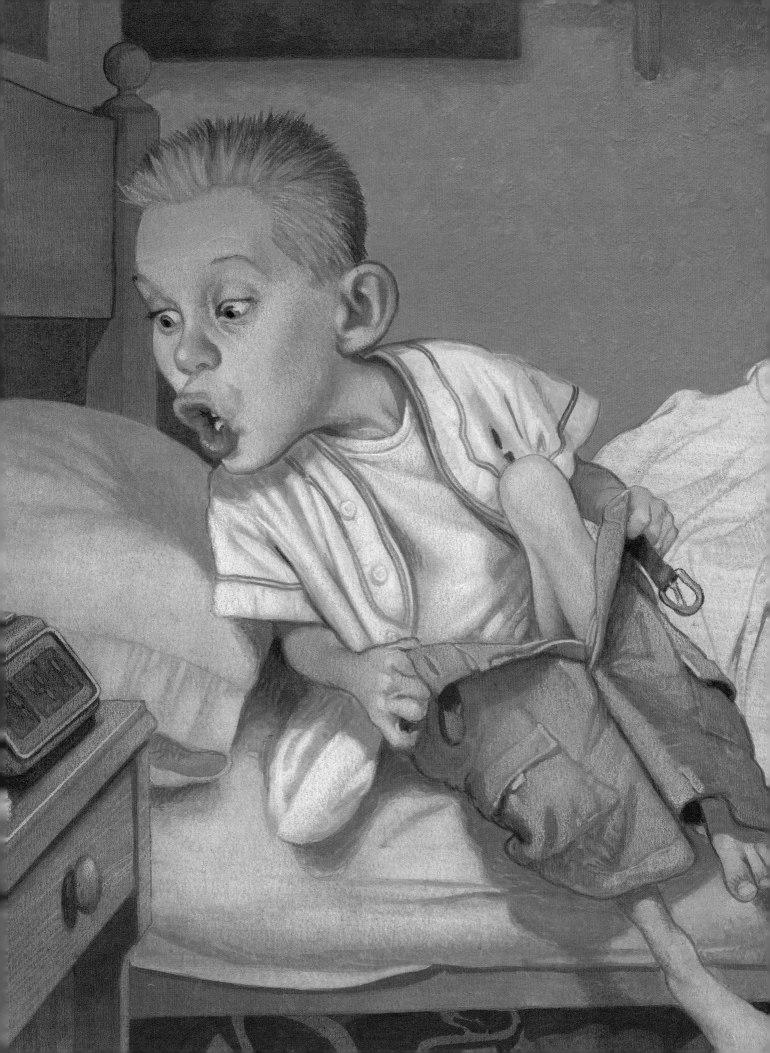

Flew down the front stair
Wet my fingers and slicked my hair
Elbowed grandma passing by
Her face went into a pie

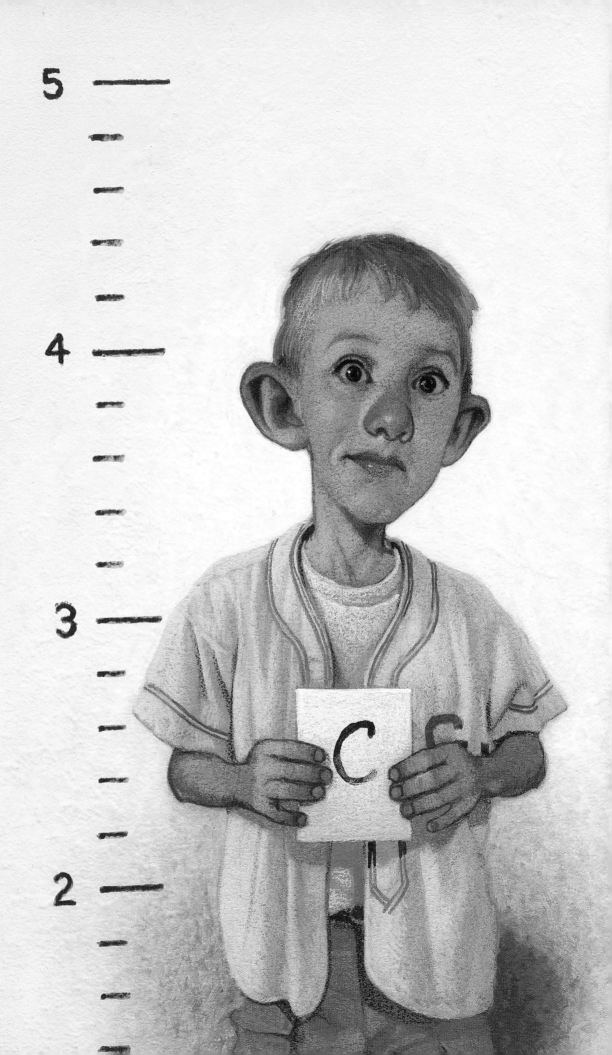

If I'm late there's misery
I won't be up on history
I'll be in the English grammar slammer
And I'll get a C!

Got a warning last semester
Told my mom and that depressed her
Promised Dad I won't be late
So gotta accelerate

Let's go!

Ran out the front door
Moving like a meteor
I sped across the front lawn quickly
Missed the bus, my shoelace tripped me

Rounded the corner
Homework flying as I go
Neighbors shouted *Tally-ho!*
And gave a standing O

Leapt across three lawn flamingos
Waved to Sal, he's Filipino
Jumped a fence and found that
I was headed toward a pool

In the air I did look funny
On TV I'd make some money
Waved my arms and legs like mad
To alter where I'd land

Whoa-*oh!*

Aimed for the rubber boat
Hit instead the kiddie float
I began to lose control
I'm so glad I learned to log roll

Jumped onto the diving board
Bounced off it and headed toward
A jungle gym, I swung just right
And caught onto a kite

Whoa! I'm flying!

Up so high I see the school
Eight a.m., that's the rule
Flying slowly, time is marking
Down below the dogs are barking

I feel like I'm sailing
But, uh-oh, the wind is failing
Now I'm headed

d
  o
    w
      n
        w
          a
            r
              d,

ground-ward,
clown-ward,
to the school

On the football field I crash
Fifty yard line, perfect smash
Grab my books and so begins
My frantic, final dash

Down the hall I ricochet
Trophy cases in the way
The other kids are all in class,
I wish that I were they

Almost
there!

I see the clock hands with delight
Eight a.m., exactly right
Pull the handle with a fight
The door is locked and that's not right

There's not a person here today
Is everybody out to play?
Now I'm thinking and it's sinking in
It's Saturday!

Aw . . .

Rats!

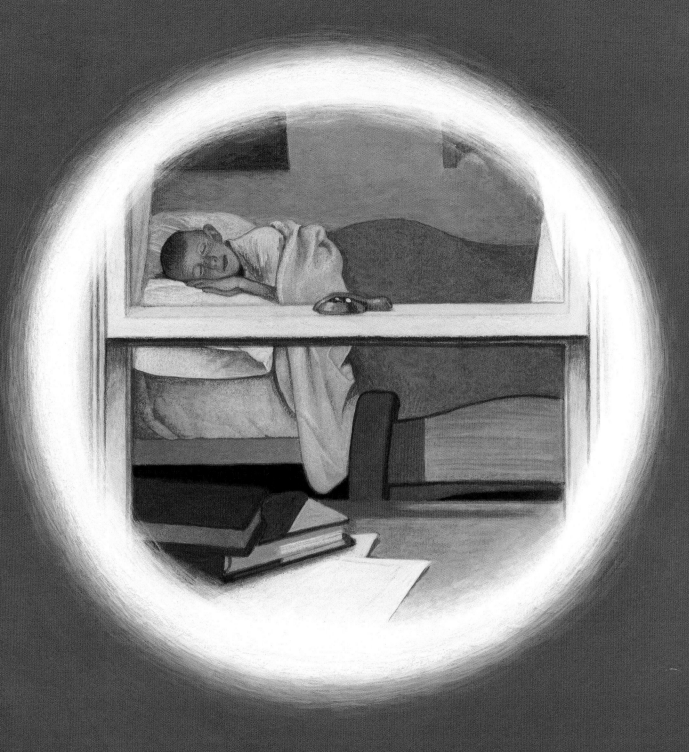

I could have stayed in bed!

I'm out the school gate
Wish that I could aviate
Or possibly evaporate
I'll be home and back in bed soon

My dad is waiting
"What the heck were you up to?
Let's go fishing, my oh my
Your grandma's face was in a pie!"

This is really something
I'm with Dad and fish are jumping
Mom gave me a new alarm
To set for Monday morn

Never want to be late for school
Never want to be the classroom fool
I'd be in the English grammar slammer
And I'd get a D!

Now my feet are doing dances
Hip-hooray for second chances
I'm not late and life is great

It's time to celebrate! *Woo!*

 Sing Along!

Woke up this morning
Clock said I was late for school
Teacher told me that's not cool
Gotta put my shirt and pants on

Flew down the front stair
Wet my fingers and slicked my hair
Elbowed grandma passing by
Her face went into a pie

If I'm late there's misery
I won't be up on history
I'll be in the English
   grammar slammer
And I'll get a C!

Got a warning last semester
Told my mom and that
   depressed her
Promised Dad I won't be late
So gotta accelerate

Let's go!

Ran out the front door
Moving like a meteor
I sped across the front lawn
   quickly
Missed the bus, my shoelace
   tripped me

Rounded the corner
Homework flying as I go
Neighbors shouted *Tally-ho!*
And gave a standing O

Leapt across three lawn flamingos
Waved to Sal, he's Filipino
Jumped a fence and found that
I was headed toward a pool

In the air I did look funny
On TV I'd make some money
Waved my arms and legs like mad
To alter where I'd land

Whoa-*oh!*

Aimed for the rubber boat
Hit instead the kiddie float
I began to lose control
I'm so glad I learned to log roll

Jumped onto the diving board
Bounced off it and headed toward
A jungle gym, I swung just right
And caught onto a kite

Whoa! I'm flying!

Up so high I see the school
Eight a.m., that's the rule
Flying slowly, time is marking
Down below the dogs are barking

I feel like I'm sailing
But, uh-oh, the wind is failing
Now I'm headed downward,
   ground-ward, clown-ward,
   to the school

On the football field I crash
Fifty yard line, perfect smash
Grab my books and so begins
My frantic, final dash

Down the hall I ricochet
Trophy cases in the way
The other kids are all in class,
I wish that I were they

Almost there!

I see the clock hands with delight
Eight a.m., exactly right
Pull the handle with a fight
The door is locked and that's
   not right

There's not a person here today
Is everybody out to play?
Now I'm thinking and it's
   sinking in
It's Saturday!

Aw...
Rats!

I could have stayed in bed!

I'm out the school gate
Wish that I could aviate
Or possibly evaporate
I'll be home and back in bed soon

My dad is waiting
"What the heck were you up to?
Let's go fishing, my oh my
Your grandma's face was in a pie!"

This is really something
I'm with Dad and fish are jumping
Mom gave me a new alarm
To set for Monday morn

Never want to be late for school
Never want to be the classroom fool
I'd be in the English
   grammar slammer
And I'd get a D!

Now my feet are doing dances
Hip-hooray for second chances
I'm not late and life is great
It's time to celebrate! *Woo!*